wag!

FWIP FWIP FWIP

• PATRICK McDONNELL •

LITTLE, BROWN AND COMPANY
Books for Young Readers
New York   Boston

This book is dedicated to my best friend, Earl.

Copyright © 2009 by Patrick McDonnell   Mutts is distributed internationally by King Features Syndicate, Inc.
All rights reserved. Except as permitted under the U.S. Copyright Act of 1976, no part of this publication may be reproduced, distributed, or transmitted
in any form or by any means, or stored in a database or retrieval system, without the prior written permission of the publisher.
Little, Brown Books for Young Readers • Hachette Book Group • 237 Park Avenue, New York, NY 10017 • Visit our Web site at www.lb-kids.com
Little, Brown Books for Young Readers is a division of Hachette Book Group, Inc. • The Little, Brown name and logo are trademarks of Hachette Book Group, Inc.
Library of Congress Cataloging-in-Publication Data: McDonnell, Patrick.   Wag / Patrick McDonnell. —1st ed.   p. cm.
Summary: Mooch the cat tries to explain what makes Earl's tail wag.
ISBN 978-0-316-04548-3   [1. Dogs—Fiction. 2. Cats—Fiction.] I. Title.
PZ7.M1554Wag 2009   [E]—dc22   2008045510
First Edition: October 2009   10 9 8 7 6 5 4 3 2 1   TTP   Printed in China   Printed on recycled paper
Book layout by Jeff Schulz / Command-Z Design

Look, there's Earl.
Shh...Let's not wake him.

Oops. He's up.
Wow! Look at his tail go....

What makes Earl's tail wag?

Well, Mooch …
What is it?

Earl's tail wags when he's eating

or playing ball

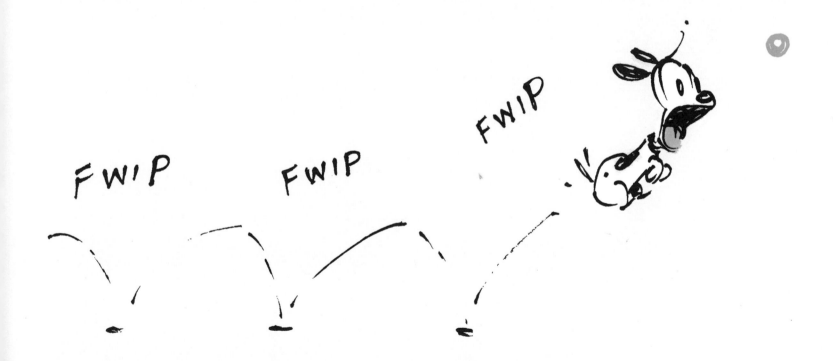

or just sitting in a field of flowers.

But what makes Earl's tail wag?

Mooch?

Now where did he go?!?

Earl's tail wags for

belly rubs,

chewy toys,

snacky-snacks,

and snowflakes.

FWIP
FWIP
FWIP

But what makes Earl's tail wag?

All right, Jules,
you tell us.

Mooch?

Earl's tail wags for friends he knows

and friends he'd like to know.

FWIP
FWIP
FWIP

It wags for his Ozzie.

Sometimes it seems to wag
for nothing at all.

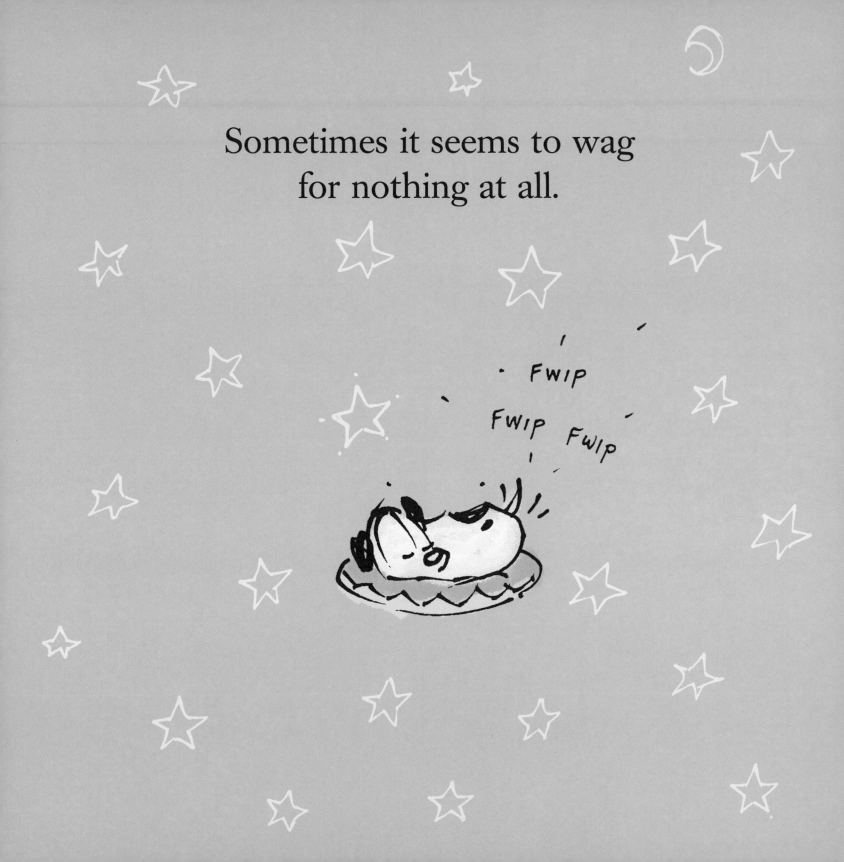

But WHAT makes Earl's tail wag?

Okay, Mooch.
Please tell us.

And of course Mooch is right.

Love is the answer.